Children's Literature Series

— 1 —

1. *The Adventurers of Crystal Lake*. Book One.

Cover: *Compugraphics* by Pierre Bertrand

THE ADVENTURERS

OF

CRYSTAL LAKE

by

Yana Amis

Best wishes
lots of fun
Y Amis

LEGAS

New York   Ottawa   Toronto

Canadian Cataloguing in Publication Data

Amis, Yana
  The Adventurers of Crystal Lake

ISBN 0-921252-85-4

I. Title.

PS8551.M58A88 1999   jC813'.54   C99-901454-1
PZ4.A5176Ad 1999

"The Adventurers of Crystal Lake" is a registered trade mark.
all images created by Yana Amis
illustrations by Yana Amis and Stirad Smolik.

For further information and for orders:

LEGAS

P. O. Box 040328	68 Kamloops Ave.	2908 Dufferin Street
Brooklyn, New York	Ottawa, Ontario	Toronto, Ontario
USA 11204	K1V 7C9	M6B 3S8

Printed and bound in Canada

.............CONTENTS

For Jake
who inspired me
to write this story

About Crystal Lake
...........and Smog Dragon

In the Country of Many Lakes there was one beautiful Crystal Lake surrounded by an ancient forest. The forest was home to many dwellers: a lazy bear, hares and hedgehogs, a cunning red fox, a proud deer, squirrels and even a wolf live there. When night falls in the forest, owls, bats, and other night creatures who are hiding during the daytime take up their posts. When the day starts butterflies and ants go about their business, and cheerful birds sing from morning to night. Busy beavers build extraordinary homes in the lake with long branches and wood sticks, which they gather from the lake shore.

In the winter the underwater inhabitants descend to the very bottom and fall asleep. Beneath the thick ice all is warm, calm, and safe. A Mermaid probably lives in the very deepest part, along with other underwater creatures. Then the winter ends and with the spring everything begins anew as it has since the dawn of time ... unless some dark force were to destroy this endless cycle of nature.

So, life on Crystal Lake was great fun for everybody until the terrible Smog Dragon took up residence on the shores of Crystal Lake and began devouring the flowers, grass and everything else within reach. Like all monsters, Smog Dragon is very sloppy and careless. He spits into the clean lake, litters it with garbage and filth, tramples the flowers and grass, and uproots saplings for no reason at all, just for his amusement. His eyes are like huge, empty windows, and a twisted, ugly chimney juts out of his body belching black smoke. This smoke blots out the sun and poisons the clean air which is precious to all living creatures and plants.

This is why Trout Gordon had to move from Crystal Lake into a fish bowl and loyal Dog Miranda and her friend Goose Steven were looking after him. Miranda was bought for a certain little boy when she was two months old. Then the boy's family moved to a new home and poor Miranda was thrown out into the street. With the last of her strength she made her way to the forest. There she found refuge for herself, met real friends and instead of a domestic pet, she became a forest dog. Goose Steven, another dweller from Crystal Lake, was forced to move from the lake into the depth of the forest because he wasn't accustomed to swimming in dirty water polluted by Smog Dragon and naturally had fallen ill. He could no longer fly because of a lung disease which sapped his strength and caused fits of coughing. The same thing happened to all the other lake and forest dwellers who hadn't already fled on foot, by wing, or by water.

After these unhappy events, the friends decided to do something about the horrible Smog Dragon who made their lives impossible.

First to speak was Trout Gordon. Sticking his head out of his fish bowl he sighed and slowly began to speak. "Friends, I am quiet by nature, but what has happened at Crystal Lake forces me to speak out. Every time Smog Dragon spits into the water a little fish dies, yet the Dragon only laughs and rumbles, "There are lots of fish in the water." If he doesn't stop soon, nothing will be left of our forest and lake."

"That's right. He is a real problem," said Goose Steven.

"We must do something about him. Get rid of him and save our Lake and forest from the dirt and pollution." Miranda wagged her tail in agreement.

"If we get rid of the Dragon, everyone will return to the forest and those who have hidden in the deepest part of the Lake will be able to swim up to the surface to admire the blue sky and green grass that I love to nibble on in the mornings."

"But how are we going to get rid of him? He is so huge. I never saw anything so huge and dangerous in my whole life?"

"That is a question we will have to find an answer to," added Trout Gordon, sticking his head up out of the water again "I also love our Lake. I'm fed up with living in a tiny fish bowl. I'm afraid I might forget how to swim in the big water."

"This is all so sad," sighed Miranda. "Let's ask Rainbow Captain for help. He's responsible for the clear sky, and the clear sky depends on the cleanliness of the earth, and the earth's cleanliness depends on the clean water and..."

"Wait Miranda," interrupted Goose Steven. He reflected for a moment, took off his baseball cap, and scratched the nape of his neck with his wing (that is the way he had brilliant thoughts), "And ... and ...," he considered, "on the earth's cleanliness depend the lives of all the birds, fishes, animals and ... people," he added hesitantly.

"Of course, people, too," observed Trout Gordon, "every single living creature."

"Oh, Steven, what a great thought that is," declared Miranda.

"Thank you my friends," said Goose Steven modestly as he straightened his bow tie. He enjoyed receiving his friends' praise and specially Miranda's for he liked her very much.

At that moment there was a low rumble that burst into a roar.

"It's Smog Dragon again," yelped Miranda, straining her neck as she tried to get a better look. She was able to see Smog Dragon slowly creeping along the lake shore, belching clouds of black smoke and making the most unbearable racket with his thundering tail. Just then a small bird fell onto the grass, overcome by the dreadful smoke and noise. The poor creature had to be rescued at once, and Miranda dashed out with Goose Steven in quick pursuit.

Gently, they picked up the bird and carried it to a safe spot. The bird appeared to have fainted at the sight of the terrible Smog Dragon and the black smoke. Goose Steven sheltered the tiny thing with his wing. Almost choking from the smoke he was desperately coughing. A frightened rabbit peeked out from behind the bushes and then quickly hopped away. A drowsy owl stuck her head out of a hollow in an ancient tree and blinked in amazement, "What's going on? What's the ruckus?" Finally, the Dragon lay down and stopped flicking its tail, bringing the uproar to an end.

The wind blew away the clouds and the sun came out again. The water in Crystal Lake grew calm. Big White Cloud hovered just above the green field. Rainbow Captain leapt off onto the ground and headed toward his friends. Rainbow Captain lived on a Tiny Star just behind the rainbow and he was riding across the sky on Big White Cloud checking to see if everything is all right in the heavens and on earth. It often rains before a rainbow

appears. This is because Rainbow Captain sprinkles fresh water across the sky making a clean path for the rainbow. (If you have not yet seen the rainbow, cheer up, for you will certainly see it one day.)

Captain was dressed in a heavenly blue suit. His multicolored hair shimmered in the sun. He was wearing special sunglasses. It would have been impossible for him to work without sunglasses for it was a very bright and hot day.

"Greetings, my friends," said Rainbow Captain in his resonant voice, "What are you discussing?"

"Greetings Captain," answered the friends.

"We are wondering how to get rid of Smog Dragon. Life is not the same on Crystal Lake any longer," said Goose Steven.

"I hate that Dragon myself," revealed Rainbow Captain. "He fouls the sky with his smoke and makes more work for me to do every day."

For a moment everyone looked at each other, then burst out in a single voice,

"Let's get rid of this no good monster!"

"All right," said Rainbow Captain thoughtfully, "there must be someone in the world who knows how to vanquish Smog Dragon." He deliberated for a moment, rubbing his chin as he gave the matter serious thought. Then Rainbow Captain nodded slowly, "I know ... we shall fly around the world and find a magic potion. Somewhere in heaven or on earth, in the forests, underwater, on a rock or deep in the jungle there must be someone or something that will help us get rid of that dreadful Smog Dragon."

"There must be a potion," chorused the friends with great excitement, "and we'll find it!"

"Pardon me," said Trout Gordon, poking his head out of the fish bowl again, "but how can I go with you on your voyage?"

"Don't worry, Gordon," said Rainbow Captain, "we'll make wheels for your fish bowl for now and after we destroy the Dragon you will swim back to Crystal Lake."

Goose Steven also expressed his concern." I am not sure if I can fly that far. I haven't been flying since I moved to the forest. I am coughing a lot from smoke and pollution and that doesn't help on a long journey."

"We will be traveling through new clean places and I promise your health will start improving as soon as we get away from here," explained Rainbow Captain.

"Then I would like to go right away," exclaimed Steven, who was suddenly stricken with a long cough.

"Oh dear," said Miranda patting him on the back. "You shouldn't get excited like this. It makes you cough. Try to speak in a quiet voice until your health improves."

"Thank you Miranda."

"But how can we all travel around the world?" she questioned.

"We'll ask Big White Cloud to be our airship," replied Rainbow Captain.

Big White Cloud was hovering nearby and heard the entire conversation.

"Of course my friends," he agreed, floating closer to the group, "I'll be your airship and your guide in the sky because I can't stand Smog Dragon and his disgusting black smoke either."

"Thank you Cloud. I knew we could count on you," continued Rainbow Captain, "So, what are we waiting for? We have no more time to lose. At dawn tomorrow, when the sun's first rays light up the sky, we'll set off on our voyage."

The friends began to prepare for the exciting journey ahead.

In Search of
..............the Magic Potion

The next morning the weather was splendid. The sun shone brightly and the lofty, clear sky opened up to embrace the travelers as they rose higher and higher on Big White Cloud. He was an experienced traveler, and no wonder, since he's flown around the world thousands of times. Our friends could see a breathtaking panorama of the earth from their great height. Far below them green valleys, blue seas, giant forests and purple mountains passed into and out of view. At one point they flew over the majestic Arctic covered with the snow and blue icebergs. As they went by, a chilling wind forced Big White Cloud to move even faster.

"Look friends," gasped Miranda, squinting from the dazzling sunlight, "the earth is a most beautiful planet. I hope that Smog Dragon will finally understand that it doesn't belong in such a remarkable world. If he wants to live on earth, he must learn to treat the land and waters with care and re- spect."

"What a deep thought," murmured Goose Steven as he attentively listened to Miranda.

Big White Cloud floated freely across the sky while the group enjoyed their flight. Rainbow Captain sat on the very edge of Cloud swinging his legs in the air. Goose Steven held his baseball cap tightly and craned his neck to watch the milky clouds float past, while Trout Gordon pressed his nose against the glass of the fish bowl through which he could see everything clearly.

Big White Cloud headed toward a towering cliff. By this time they had traveled thousands of miles from Crystal Lake. On this rocky cliff lived an ancient Bald Eagle who possessed great wisdom and knowledge. The friends had sought him out to ask where they could find the magic potion that would rid them of the terrible Smog Dragon. Suddenly, the wind grew stronger, the sky became overcast and thunder rolled ominously above the heads of the carefree travelers.

"Friends, a storm is coming," cried Big White Cloud anxiously, "I'll set you beneath an overhang on the cliff which will shelter you from the weather."

The wind grew more fierce and black, angry clouds encircled Big White Cloud, but he maneuvered* skillfully and gently descended to a safe overhang on the cliff. Our friends hopped off the Cloud and he floated upwards to the highest spot in the sky where he usually hid from threatening winds and rain.

As the adventurers peered out from beneath their shelter, they noticed a solitary, mighty oak tree. At the oak's summit the Bald Eagle had made his nest within the crown formed by the branches. The companions dashed out from their ledge and spread themselves out beneath the oak tree, where they were protected by the dense foliage from the wind and rain. The Bald Eagle noticed his visitors and decided to make their acquaintance. Opening his broad, strong wings he gracefully swooped down to the ground, landing at the astonished friends' feet.

"Greetings," said Bald Eagle, What has brought you to my domain?"

Dumbfounded by the majesty of their host, the friends were unable to find their voices. Goose Steven backed into the shadow of the foliage, his wing covering the fish bowl where sleepy Trout Gordon knew nothing of what was happening. Rainbow Captain stepped forward, "Greetings Bald Eagle. We are from Crystal Lake. I am Rainbow Captain and these are my friends, Miranda (Miranda wagged her tail in greeting), our respected Goose Steven (Steven gave an elegant bow), and in the fish bowl, if you look closely, is our dear friend Trout Gordon. We flew here on Big White Cloud, brought by great misfortune on this long journey."

Bald Eagle studied the entire group with his omniscient gaze.

"What kind of misfortune?"

"A terrible Smog Dragon has settled near our Crystal Lake, strewing debris over the lake and forest, poisoning the fresh air with his toxic breath and fouling the clear water in the lake. We fear this Dragon and want to get rid of him, but we don't know how to do it. We came to you wise Eagle to ask for some advice"

20

After a few moments, Bald Eagle gravely addressed the group. "I've heard about Smog Dragon, my friends. A flock of wild geese who had flown over Crystal Lake told me about him. I'm very sorry, but I can't do anything to help you because I've grown older and I'm not as strong as I was many years ago. But I can offer you some advice. In the middle of the Atlantic Ocean you will find Merry Dolphin. Dolphins are very intelligent creatures, and I'll tell you something else. This one is so clever he understands even human language."

"I understand human language, too," blurted Miranda, "sometimes I think it would be better if I didn't understand people because they say such confusing things."

"So," continued Bald Eagle, "go and find Merry Dolphin. He may be able to help you."

"Thank you, we're very grateful for your advice," replied the friends. Just then, the sun peeked out from behind the clouds and everything became brighter.

"Look," exclaimed Goose Steven joyfully, "here's Big White Cloud again." Big White Cloud wafted down close to the ground.

"Come on," said Rainbow Captain, "we don't have a moment to lose. We must get going."

"Where are we going?" asked Big White Cloud.

"To the Atlantic Ocean."

"Oh, that's very far. But with the wind's help we'll make it," finished Cloud optimistically.

"Let's go!" cried the friends seating themselves comfortably on Big White Cloud.

And in no time they were off in search of Merry Dolphin.

New Places
.............and New Friends

My friend, if you look at any world map or a globe, you will see the color blue everywhere. This blue is the color of water, the color of the seas and oceans spreading across our entire planet. Blue is also the color of clear, tranquil skies. If you stand on the ocean shore and look into the distance where the water meets the sky, you will see an unbroken line. This line is called the horizon. If you are on a ship and you sail toward the horizon, the sea appears to expand and new horizons open up before you, and so on to infinity*, because horizons at sea, just as in life, are endless. Those who discover and reach out toward new horizons are the happiest creatures in the world.

Our adventurers also reached the horizon many times and every time they did so they thought that they had reached the shores of the ocean but instead a new expanse of water and sky opened up ahead of them and so it went for many days. Finally Big White Cloud with his passengers descended to the water's surface. Looking as far as the eye could see, they scanned the ocean for the sight of Merry Dolphin.

However, finding him in the endless blue was not easy. The day was drawing to a close with the sun hanging low on the horizon like an enormous orange. The sky turned from blue to purple, the ocean to a dark green and Big White Cloud took on a lavender tint. At sunset all nature changes color, as if discarding her daytime clothing and changing into an evening dress of unusual beauty.

23

"How can we find Merry Dolphin in such a big ocean?" queried Goose Steven spreading his wings in perplexity.

"Let's call out to him together," suggested Miranda.

"Good idea," agreed Rainbow Captain, "Ready? One, two, three."

"MERRY DOLPHIN!" they shouted, "WHERE ARE YOU MERRY DOLPHIN?"

They fell silent and waited expectantly. No response came, the silence broken only by the gently lapping of the waves.

"I know how we can find Merry Dolphin," announced Trout Gordon, "It's my turn to help."

Trout Gordon leapt out of his fish bowl and dove into the unfamiliar, salty water. Several minutes passed, but Gordon did not return.

"He probably swam away out of joy and we'll never see him again," sighed Big White Cloud.

"May be he got lost," suggested Miranda.

At that very moment Trout Gordon appeared at the water's surface.

"Friends, I'm so happy to be swimming in the ocean. I'll find Merry Dolphin and bring him back with me. Wait for us here." Then he vanished into the water again.

Rainbow Captain, Miranda and Goose Steven sat down close together on cushiony Big White Cloud, and waited for Gordon's return.

Night settled over the ocean. It grew dark and the temperature dropped. Big White Cloud rose above the water and began to rock from side to side. The travelers were so tired that their eyes closed immediately and soon they were lulled into a peaceful sleep. As night deepened, Big White Cloud became almost invisible.

* * *

The next morning the traveling companions awoke to the singing of Merry Dolphin. Trout Gordon was circling in the water nearby.

"Wake up friends," yelped Miranda. Rainbow Captain arose and stretched himself. Goose Steven opened his eyes and stretched his wings. Big White Cloud awoke abruptly and drifted down almost to the water's surface.

"Look," shouted Rainbow Captain with delight, "it must be Trout Gordon and Merry Dolphin!"

By way of greeting, Merry Dolphin leapt out of the water, flipped in mid-air and broke the ocean's smooth surface with a playful splash.

"I'm very pleased to meet you all. Trout Gordon told me about Smog Dragon who has poisoned the lives of the inhabitants of Crystal Lake. I'm sorry, but I'm afraid I can't help you. However, I can advise you who to ask for help."

"That would be great," said Rainbow Captain.

"Well," began Merry Dolphin slowly and then, after diving into the water one more time, he continued, " I'm not familiar with the earth's surface, but if it has anything to do with the ocean," he paused in thought, "What is the name of that place where the palm trees grow, where crocodiles are found and the grass is as tall as men?"

"You mean the jungle, my friend," suggested Big White Cloud.

"That's right, the jungle," exclaimed Merry Dolphin, leaping with joy.

Some water sprayed Goose Steven, who had been preening his feathers . He looked up, "What's in the jungle? And where is the jungle?"

"In the jungle," resumed Merry Dolphin, "live...oh, it's slipped my mind, you know, those funny, furry creatures that live in palm trees, eat bananas and look like human beings."

"You're thinking of monkeys, my friend," offered Big White Cloud, floating so low above the Dolphin's head that Rainbow Captain got his boots wet and Miranda hastily clambered into the very middle of the Cloud to avoid falling in.

"I didn't know," remarked Merry Dolphin, "that a cloud could be so learned. I always thought that clouds were light and airy with no real substance."

26

"Some are like that," observed Big White Cloud dryly, "it all depends on their experience. I've been around the world a thousand times."

"And I've crossed the ocean a thousand times," returned Merry Dolphin.

"Yes," continued Big White Cloud, "but the world doesn't end with the ocean."

"The world doesn't end with the sky either," suggested Dolphin.

"The world never ends. The world is endless as far as I can understand it," interjected Rainbow Captain.

"Friends," Miranda hastened, "stop debating. Please continue, Merry Dolphin."

Merry Dolphin collected his thoughts.

"Somewhere, not far from the jungles of the Silver River, lives Zaki the Golden Lion. He knows everything in the world because he has animals and birds that report everything to him that occurs, not only in the jungle, but in nature all over the world. I heard about Zaki the Golden Lion from Flying Fish, who vacationed here last season. I think Zaki will help you."

"Looks like we are getting back on the right track thanks to you Merry Dolphin." said Captain,

"By the way I have been looking at you and there is something I don't understand. Your skin looks terribly dirty for a creature who spends all his life in the water. Looks like your skin is covered in some greasy stuff. What is it?"

Merry Dolphin nodded in agreement, "That's exactly what it is, greasy stuff. It's oil. Did you ever hear about oil spills? Huge oil tankers which are cruising the oceans spill oil all over the place. Other ships also carelessly spill fuel and dump wastes in the ocean. It is very bad for us, because we can not wash it off. The sea food gets poisoned and it makes us sick. So marine mammals, fish, sea birds and other marine creatures are dying from this garbage. At least I am still alive. A lot of my friends are dead or crippled because of the oil spills, and other trash brought here by people."

The friends looked at each other.

"Sounds just like our Dragon."

"It's even worse here because you have only one Dragon. At sea there are thousands off ships and vessels going day and night and no one stops them?'

"Well, why don't we wash Merry Dolphin, my friends?" exclaimed cheerful Miranda.

"What do you say Dolphin? Would you like us to try to wash the greasy oil off your skin?" asked Rainbow Captain.

"I would love to have a real bath! I miss my clean looks. I can't clean myself all over because I don't have hands as you can see, just fins."

"All right friends, let's get busy."

Big White Cloud then descended as low as possible over the water. Trout Gordon dove to the depths and in a few minutes returned with a bunch of fresh seaweed.

"Here is the soap," he said passing the seaweed to Rainbow Captain and went back for more. He returned holding in his teeth a light ocean sponge. "Here is the brush."

Dolphin pressed as closely as he could to Cloud so that Captain and Miranda could reach his face and back. Captain spread seaweed all over Dolphin's body and using the sponge he started rubbing Dolphin's skin, gradually increasing pressure.

"Oh, that feels so good," cried the happy Dolphin, "no one ever gave me a bath before. That feels great!" Dolphin's skin began looking brighter and cleaner. He dove into the water to rinse himself off and reappeared on the surface all shiny and sparkling clean.

"Come closer. Now you look yourself again," said Miranda with a broad smile.

"Do you know that your skin is the color of water?" Goose Steven remarked.

"And the color of sky," added Big White Cloud happily. "Look, he has a white chest. Before the bath we couldn't see it. It was covered by grimy oil."

"I wish I had a mirror to look at my new clean self," said the exuberant Dolphin.

"You look swell friend, trust me," reassured Trout Gordon, who was as excited as Merry Dolphin.

"Look into my eyes," invited Miranda, "and you will see your new clean self reflection in them."

Dolphin did just that.

"Indeed I can see. I look smaller, but I can see my new clean self very well, and I love it. Now I can approach the pretty Dolphiness, and invite her for an ocean social" he said with a big smile

"Thank you ever so much"

"You're welcome," answered the friends. "It's too bad we are too late to help others who were killed by the dirt and pollution."

"Friends," called Trout Gordon as he swam up to the water's surface, "I have something important to tell you."

"What is it?"

Rainbow Captain, Miranda and Big White Cloud watched Gordon as he hesitated for a while before breaking the news.

"I've decided to stay in the ocean. I feel much more at home here, and

I'm afraid I wouldn't be able to stand a long trip in a fish bowl," explained Gordon.

"I knew it was coming," remarked Cloud.

"What do you think friends?" Captain addressed the crew.

"Well, it's his choice" responded Miranda.

"I agree," nodded Steven

"Me too," sighed Big White Cloud.

"Well," Rainbow Captain said as he turned to the small fish, "Good luck in the new water Gordon."

"I'll miss you."

"We'll miss you too."

And so the friends all bade Trout Gordon farewell*. Then, without further ado, Big White Cloud lifted upwards, carrying Rainbow Captain, Miranda and Goose Steven off toward new adventures.

NO MY FRIEND

YOU HAVE NOT MADE A MISTAKE

THIS IS A TRULY DARK PAGE

AS YOU SEE

THE SUN

HAS NOT GLANCED THIS WAY

EVEN ONCE

AND THEREFORE NOTHING CAN BE SEEN

THIS IS WHAT BECAME OF

CRYSTAL LAKE

WHILE OUR FRIENDS WERE TRAVELING

IN SEARCH OF A MAGIC POTION

SMOG DRAGON

POISONED

THE FRESH AIR

AND DARKENED THE SKY

WITH HIS BLACK BREATH

AND LIFE ALMOST STOPPED

AT
CRYSTAL LAKE

In the
........................Jungle

From birds flying by, our friends learned about the worsening conditions at their beloved lake and Big White Cloud sped up with all his might leaving thousands and thousands miles behind. Although he was an experienced traveler, even he could not have imagined how difficult it would be to reach the jungle. He had to journey almost around the entire planet.

Several times Big White Cloud unexpectedly fell into air pockets. What is more, the air at high altitude being very cold, made our friends shiver. It seemed to them as if they were swimming in a huge glass of cold milk.

Traveling over large cities also was a challenge. Almost every major city of the world was covered by the pollution and heavy industrial smoke. It looked as though Smog Dragon had been almost everywhere. At times the adventurers' eyes would turn pink and teary and poor Goose Steven started coughing again.

Finally, when thousands and thousands of miles, countless countries and cities, lakes, seas, mountains and forests lay behind them, the flight over the ocean's sparkling expanses and many strange lands was finished. Big White Cloud dropped lower and our friends warmed themselves beneath the sun's hot rays. They viewed the panorama that opened up before their eyes. Down below stretched the wide Silver River.

The jungle surrounding the Silver River not only stretches along its banks, but it also forms vast green islands in the center. Some of the islands looked bare naked because there were no trees or any living creatures there at all. These bald spots of empty land stretched miles and miles through the jungle and from the air looked like enormous dirty pancakes.

"Look at the bald spots," exclaimed Miranda. "I wonder what that is?"

"Looks like the forest here was almost shaved by some powerful machinery or may be it was destroyed by an alien force from another planet," suggested Rainbow Captain.

"Why would they do something like this?" asked Steven.

"Who knows. May be they just hate the Earth's nature."

Big White Cloud was coming closer to the green mass of the jungle.

"Oh, this fresh smell makes me think of Crystal Lake," said Miranda.

"This air is good. It definitely clears my throat," agreed Goose Steven inhaling the deeply sweet fragrance of exotic fruits and flowers.

Like Crystal Lake and its ancient forest, the jungle is a home to many animals, exotic birds, and plants. In the river itself live fish and underwater animals rarely seen and on the surface grow pink and white lilies and other thick jungle vegetation. Sticking their heads up out of the water, giant crocodiles lazily bask in the sun and gigantic orange frogs can be seen leaping here and there.

In the jungle, monkeys call back and forth to each other and smart parrots fly from tree to tree. Coconut and banana trees grow here, as do breadfruit trees, rubber plants and fishtail palms.

Elephants come to the Silver River day and night to freshen up and bathe wounds received in fights with enemies or in playful fighting. Their favorite song is:

If you ever get a fever
Get yourself to Silver River
Get yourself here quick and fast
And your fever will have past

Big White Cloud hung low over the unknown territory and the travelers, their heads spinning from the long flight, jumped down onto the ground.

"I think I will stroll across the sky until a tropical rain falls. This spot is famous for its tropical showers. Why don't all of you take a rest?" advised Big White Cloud.

Freed from the weight of his passengers, Cloud floated up lightly and disappeared from their view.

"Hi," said a friendly voice. The friends looked up, but could see nothing but the heavy branches of liana vines* and palm trees.

"Over here." Suddenly, they saw a monkey hanging upside down, his tail wrapped around a palm branch. "Welcome," sang the lively monkey as he playfully leapt to another tree followed by his brothers and sisters.

Goose Steven had never seen monkeys before. He stretched his head so far out that his baseball cap fell onto the grass. Just then, long-legged Pink Flamingo appeared. She picked up the cap and held it out toward Goose Steven. Without taking his eyes away from the beautiful Flamingo, he jammed his cap back onto his head.

"Thank you. You are very kind," whispered Goose Steven, shyly.

"Oh!" quipped Pink Flamingo with her full, vibrant voice, "You're welcome. Why are you looking at me as if you want to eat me. Don't forget that you and I belong to the same family, namely birds. Incidentally, I am from a very good family and inherited my fine pink plumage from my Grandmother, Countess Flamingo."

Goose Steven was astonished. Never before had he spoken to such an elevated personage. He opened his beak in wide amazement and flapped his eyelids.

"Countess," said Rainbow Captain, bowing deeply, "please excuse my friend, he is simply overwhelmed by your beauty."

"Oh, how charming you are," preened Pink Flamingo. She went on in bewitching merriment, "Welcome to our green kingdom. We are very much in need of the company of gentlemen here. Unfortunately, neither the hippopotamus nor the rhinoceros are elegant, nor are they known for their fine manners. Be careful with the crocodiles and don't get too close to the water. These beasts have no conscience. They will eat anyone at all and only think about their own stomachs. Just take a look at their wide open mouths and saber-sharp teeth."

"They must have a good dentist," commented Miranda, keeping up the social chit-chat.

"Oh, I don't doubt that for a moment," answered Pink Flamingo wryly.

"Tell us dear, what are those ugly bald spots stretching through your jungle and the river islands. We noticed it from the air?" continued curious Miranda.

"Oh," sighed Pink Flamingo, "men went there and cut thousands of our trees. Imagine! All the creatures had to flee of course. Who wants to live in an empty space? You will find it quite crowded here because they all moved into our territory. Specially on the shores of the river.

Many of them are dead now. Poor things could never get used to the new place. Before that happened everyone knew its own home. Now it's a terrible mess. We are already short of food and water. If they continue chopping our jungle like crazy we are not going to have a place to live. It is as simple as that." She sighed again.

"Oh, dear. What will happened then?" asked a very concerned Miranda.

"The jungle will be doomed to sickness and death as far as I can see."

"Sounds familiar," said Rainbow Captain. "We are ourselves trying to find a potion to kill Smog Dragon who lives at our home at Crystal Lake."

"Smog Dragon!" exclaimed Pink Flamingo. "Never heard of such a beast. What is it? An animal, a bird? Where did he come from."

"We don't know. He just appeared on the shores of Crystal Lake and made it his home without our invitation. He pollutes the air, poisons the environment,* damages our forest and terrorizes our animals and birds. He is a life threatening monster and we have to get rid of him or we are going to be dead ourselves," said Rainbow Captain.

"Did you try to vanquish him somehow?"

"We can't do that alone. He is a huge stinking beast. It will take a magic potion to solve this problem and we intend to find it."

"Well, I wish you all the luck in the world" said Pink Flamingo.

All at once, an enormous snake emerged from the high grass and fixing his hungry eyes on the chatting friends, slithered menacingly toward them.

"Careful!" cried the monkey from above, swinging excitedly from one branch to another. "Careful!" he shouted again, "look behind you! That's Dreaded Python!"

Startled, Pink Flamingo ran off at high speed to hide. The Python continued his stealthy advance and Goose Steven trembling with fear hid behind Rainbow Captain. Sensing the danger, Miranda barked and growled, her body quivering as if she were about to shoot an arrow. (Don't forget my friend, she was truly a very courageous dog.) Nearer and nearer the Python approached. Rainbow Captain and Miranda prepared to fight him. As he drew closer to the travelers, Dreaded Python spoke in a slow drawl.

"If yo...u ha.a.ave co..ome he..re, it wa..sn..'t so tha..t I cou..ld ea..t yo..u, so.. wh..y ha..ve yo..u co..o.me to.. the... jungle?"

"We are here on a very important mission," declared Rainbow Captain fearlessly.

"I..am no..t at a..ll inte..r.e..st..ed in.. yo..ur bus..i.ne..ss," hissed the Python ominously, "It's lu..nch ti..me and I wou..ld lo..ve to ea..t this de..lic..ious bi..rd," and the Python charged toward Goose Steven. Poor Steven clutched at Rainbow Captain in terror.

"Don't you dare even think about it!" Miranda snarled loudly as she lunged toward the Python.

Cautiously, the Python began to retreat just as Rainbow Captain lifted a heavy stone and threw it at the Python's eyes. The monkey pulled a coconut from the top of a palm tree and threw it down onto the Python's head.

"That should cool you off!" he chortled triumphantly.

The Python closed his injured eye and, frowning in pain, slithered off to one side to nurse his wounds. He grumbled angrily: "Ju...st thi..nk, all sorts of stran...gers co..me he..re and tr..y to ma..ke the..ir own ru..les ri..ght aw..ay.

I'll br..ing th.is up for dis..cu..ssion at the next J..ungle Co..mmittee mee..ting."

It was then that our friends felt a warm, soft puff of air from above.

"What's going on here?" asked Big White Cloud , "I was enjoying myself studying the surroundings when a blue parrot caught up with me and warned me that you were in danger. I've hurried back to get you out of here. Get up on my back and we'll set off in search of Zaki The Golden Lion."

Following his advice, our friends swiftly clambered up onto Big White Cloud. As he lifted up high into the sky, Goose Steven sighed in relief, "To tell the truth, I feel much safer in the air than on the ground."

"We gave Dreaded Python a good thrashing!" laughed Rainbow Captain.

"He deserved it," Miranda chimed in, "and did you see how quickly Pink Flamingo got away? I hoped she would stay and help us to fight this no good Python."

"She got scared and ran away for her life," said Rainbow Captain.

"I think that some elevated personages don't have what it takes to fight evil," concluded Big White Cloud.

"She seemed to be quite charming," said Goose Steven.

"Charming doesn't mean brave, my friend," responded Cloud.

"Really?"

"Trust me. I've flown around the world and I know what I am talking about," Big White Cloud finished with confidence.

And so they continued their voyage in search of new adventures.

In the Land of
.........Zaki the Golden Lion

The sun slipped rapidly beneath the horizon and, as always happens in the tropics, the dark, velvety night fell immediately. Bright stars appeared in the sky and began to twinkle cheerfully at each other and the whole world. The stars in these parts hang so low, it almost seems as if you could touch them with your hand. However, the fact is they are several millions of light years away. It is very far my friend.

The bright moon lit up the way for our travelers like a large flashlight. Big White Cloud found his way easily in the night and flew in the right direction — far southward where lay the land of Zaki the Golden Lion. Only as morning approached did the tired Cloud deliver the friends from Crystal Lake to their destination. By this time they were thousands and thousands of miles away from home.

*   *   *

Zaki the Golden Lion was an old animal, a survivor who had outwitted many a hunter and thwarted countless attacks by his enemies. Once he was captured by hunters of exotic animals who hoped to sell him to one of the world's zoos. Zaki was very strong then. He escaped by chewing through the wooden bars of the cage the hunters had locked him in. Since that time Zaki had secluded himself from the cares of the world and lived in his own land where Cat Lawrence acted as his steward and secretary.

No one knew how Cat Lawrence had come to this part of the world-only that he had been living there a very long time and felt himself at home. He was regarded highly for his knowledge. Other animals often came to him with questions and requests. They reported all their important news to him, which he then reported in turn to Zaki the Golden Lion. Cat Lawrence had long whiskers and he moved with composure. Every morning Lawrence made breakfast for Zaki the Golden Lion and delivered a written account of the happenings in nature and the animal world. He also took care of the cactus garden and performed other domestic chores. On this particular morning, he finished his chores earlier than usual and eagerly prepared for his daily walk.

By this time, Big White Cloud had landed in the territory of Zaki the Golden Lion. Goose Steven, still frightened by his encounter with the Python, did not want to step onto the ground.

It was very quiet there and Miranda pricked up her ears attentively.

"We're probably in the wrong place," wailed Goose Steven, his head hanging down from the Cloud as he peered around.

It was just at this time that Cat Lawrence had set off on his walk. The companions gaped in silent wonder as they watched a big, black cat come out of a nearby cave. An ID card hung around the cat's neck and a gleaming watch was strapped to his paw.

"Who's making so much noise out here?" he meowed irritably.

He came to an abrupt stop when he saw Miranda and Rainbow Captain. As he studied them from head to toe he spoke briskly. "Are you the police?"

"No, we are not," replied Rainbow Captain. "We are..."

"In that case, what is this dog doing here and how did you find Zaki the

Golden Lion's residence?" interrupted cat. "His address is unlisted. Zaki does not like being disturbed."

"We have a good reason," said Rainbow Captain.

"I would like to hear about it."

"Dear Cat ..."

"My name is Cat Lawrence," declared the cat pointing at his ID. card proudly, "and everyone knows that around here."

"Oh, we beg your pardon," began Miranda humbly, "no one in our land heard about you ever."

"Mmmm. I find it surprising. So, what has brought you to these distant parts?" meowed Cat Lawrence, pleasantly sunning himself.

"We live at Crystal Lake, which is at the other end of the earth in the Land of Many Lakes."

"Oh, I heard it's a beautiful land. How did you make your way here?" purred Cat Lawrence.

"We flew here on our friend."

Cat Lawrence looked surprised, "What do you mean?"

Rainbow Captain pointed a finger over his head and Cat Lawrence looked up in astonishment. Big White Cloud smiled down at him from his comfortable position on the treetop.

"A very interesting means of transportation! And who is that cowering over there?" he asked, having noticed Goose Steven.

"That is our friend, Goose Steven," explained Miranda.

"Very interesting," purred Lawrence softly. After a short pause, he regained his businesslike manner. "So, what has happened at Crystal Lake?"

Rainbow Captain took up the story. "At our lake, Smog Dragon has come to live. He pollutes the sky with his black breath, he poisons the water in the lake and he has killed many forest animals and creatures living in the water. Our other friend, Trout Gordon, was forced to live in a fish bowl because the water in the Lake is so polluted by the Dragon and Steven got lung disease and can't fly any longer."

Cat Lawrence was shocked. "The poor fish has to live in a fish bowl? And you can't fly any longer?" He cast a sympathetic glance at Steven.... "What a terrible monster this Smog Dragon is. I hope you are going to do something about him"

"We are trying to," said Rainbow Captain, "but we do not know how to chase him away.

We can't do it alone, he is too big and strong. You know, he's a real monster!"

"Oh... I see. Hmm... you must have help. I will try to arrange a meeting with Zaki the Golden Lion. I think he will be able to find a solution for you."

"That would be so kind of you."

"Please do something," implored Big White Cloud, "because personally, I shall never go back to Crystal Lake as long as this dirty monster is there, covering everything with smoke."

"All right," said Cat Lawrence "I will take care of it. In the meantime, why don't you go for a walk and enjoy the fresh air?" Then Lawrence sauntered off.

"Shall we go for a walk? I love exploring new places," said Rainbow Captain.

"This place looks a little like Crystal Lake. Look at the tall green grass. I would like to know how things are going at home," sniffled Miranda.

"Soon we shall find out," replied Rainbow Captain. "Hey, Goose Steven, you can step onto the ground. There are no pythons here."

Big White Cloud lowered himself and Goose Steven stepped onto the ground. Rainbow Captain purposefully strode off into the tall, thick grass. Miranda loyally followed, sniffing and smelling the unfamiliar odors of the land. They discovered unusual plants and insects. Butterflies flitted from flower to flower and the birds sang their happy songs. With great interest they took in the new surroundings forgetting for a while about the hardship of the journey and the misfortune that had brought them to this strange land so distant from their home.

"By the way, where did Steven go?"

"Steven, where are you?" barked Miranda. But the only response was a rustling in the grass.

"Steven, please answer!" they called, but again without result.

"Something has happened to him. This way," Miranda led, darting off to her right, "here are his small tracks. Follow me Captain."

They went off into the deep grass, where they found themselves facing the entrance to an underground cave.

"He's somewhere here, I can smell him."

Without hesitation they stepped inside the cave. Rainbow Captain's hair fluorescing in the darkness was the only source of light. The passage way was narrow and from time to time they bumped into stalactites* which were like stone icicles hung from the roof and stumbled over stalagmites* which

were sticking out of the floor like giant teeth. An insect landed on Rainbow Captain's face and he furiously whisked it away. Miranda then took the lead sniffing her way along.

"Steven, where are you?" called Rainbow Captain.

"I'm here, I'm here," came a small whisper from the darkness.

"What happened to you?"

"I was just sniffing the flowers and touching the grass. I wandered into this cave and found myself trapped. Don't come any closer, or you will also find yourselves imprisoned by this monster."

By then Rainbow Captain's eyes had grown accustomed to the darkness and he saw the monster lying in a corner, looking like a huge gray jellyfish. Trembling in the monster's grip was little Goose Steven. Miranda barked and the monster awoke. He opened first one eye, then the other, and looking longingly at the travelers, he asked, "Are you intruders from outside? I've never seen you here before." He spoke slowly in deep tones.

"That's right, and we have come to free our friend," challenged Rainbow Captain boldly, "but first tell me this, what are you doing here?"

"I live here."

"What's your name?"

"My name is Cave Watcher. I guard this cave and I never go outside. I mustn't go out into the sun because I have lived my whole life in the darkness."

"Oh," began Goose Steven, who had been silent with terror until now, "at Crystal Lake where we live, I have an owl for a friend who has also never seen the daylight."

"Is that really true?" asked Cave Watcher, and in his excitement he opened his paws.

Taking advantage of this lapse, Goose Steven squirmed out of his grasp and rushed to his friends.

"How interesting," mused Cave Watcher, "I always thought that I was the only one who could not see in the light."

"Oh no, there are a great many such creatures in the world," said Rainbow Captain helpfully.

Cave Watcher nodded his huge head in disbelief.

"You're joking."

"It's the absolute truth," assured Miranda.

"You know," said Cave Watcher, "I really like you. And by the way," he turned to Goose Steven, "I did not mean to do you any harm. I just wanted to have a friend. I am very lonely in this cave, you know."

"I understand," said Goose Steven.

"I've been living in this cave a hundred years," continued Cave Watcher, "and I have never had a real friend."

Recovering from his terror, Goose Steven began to feel sorry for Cave Watcher who had never been to the outside world and never had a real friend. He scratched the nape of his neck with his wing (this was the way he had brilliant thoughts), and said. "I will ask a bird of some kind to fly in to you every morning and sing songs for you. Would you like that?"

"Oh!" exclaimed Cave Watcher, "Would I like that? Of course! No one has ever sung songs for me. I am delighted!" And Cave Watcher jumped with joy for the first time in a hundred years.

"I would like to do something for you, can I help you somehow?"

"We are waiting for a meeting with Zaki the Golden Lion and we don't want to be late," said Rainbow Captain, "tell us how to get out from the cave fast."

"That's simple. Follow this path until you reach an underground stalactite cave. There you will find a long passageway, go straight ahead until you see the sunlight. The bats use this exit, also." He whistled, and a tiny bat crash landed from the ceiling almost hitting him on the nose.

"When are you going to learn to land properly?" asked Cave Watcher.

"Never. That's the way I like it," she said. "Now, what can I do for you?"

"Nothing for me. But I want you to show my guests the way out."

"Oh, now you want me to help you after saying you don't have any friends. I heard you, you know."

"How can you say we are friends, we're fighting all the time?"

"So, what are friends for?"

"How can bats recognize their friends," interjected Miranda, "I thought they were blind."

"Bats can see neither in the dark nor the light" said Rainbow Captain.

"Hey, easy on the bats pal. I don't need eyes to see. I use my fine ears instead. We can do without seeing as much as you can with your no-good-in-the-darkness eyes."

"There is no need to be rude," Cave Watcher pointed out, slightly embarrassed.

"I am not rude. I am just telling it like it is. Can't you stand the truth?"

"Please go," pleaded Cave Watcher.

"Good by Cave Watcher. Thank you for your help," said Rainbow Captain.

"Good by. I'll miss you all," he said weeping softly.

"We'll miss you, too," said the friends sincerely.

"Oh, please stop feeling sorry for him. The old bag is used to being alone. He has been sitting here for a hundred years. Personally, I could never understand what prevented him from moving his butt toward the entrance? Even us bats get out once in while."

"Shut up bat," shouted Cave Watcher losing his patience. "What do you know about the loneliness and fear of venturing out into the unknown?"

"See, he thinks if he is a senior he can scream at me. Isn't it the worst case of discrimination?"

"Please, let's get going," pleaded Miranda.

"OK, let's get going," agreed the disagreeable bat.

"Cheer up," Steven encouraged Cave Watcher "We'll send you a song bird, I promise."

"Good," bat said, "May be that will get him off my case."

Following the tiny bat, in no time they found themselves outside.

"Oh, there you are," said Big White Cloud, "where did you disappear to? I've been looking everywhere for you." He was hanging low, almost touching the high grass in the middle of the field that faced the back entrance of the cave.

"It's my fault," sighed Goose Steven, "I got lost in an underground cave where we met a lonely Cave Watcher."

"I'm sorry I wasn't with you. I've never seen a Cave Watcher."

"That's because he never comes outside," said Miranda.

"Is that right? On the other hand, I've never been in an underground cave," Big White Cloud shrugged, "to each his own as they say. So friends, let's be on our way. Cat Lawrence has made an appointment for us with Zaki the Golden Lion and we better be on time."

*   *   *

They hurried off to meet Cat Lawrence for their audience with Zaki the Golden Lion.

As they stopped near the Lion's dwelling, Cat Lawrence turned to Big White Cloud: "Please be so good as to wait over here. In Zaki's cave there is not enough room for clouds and other unidentified flying objects."

Cloud sighed with disappointment.

"We won't go in without Cloud. He is not an unidentified flying object he is our friend."

"That's right," joined Goose Steven supportively.

"We can't leave Cloud outside, it's unfair," insisted Miranda, "If it weren't for him, we could never have flown here."

"Me..ow," noted Cat Lawrence, "what rare solidarity. I will allow it just this once."

"I'll make myself smaller," offered Big White Cloud, cheering up. Then he shrank to almost half his regular size.

"Please follow me," instructed Lawrence, "and remember, in Zaki's presence speak loudly. Don't interrupt and don't ask silly questions."

"We have good manners," replied Miranda. "At Crystal Lake everyone is very well brought up."

"All right then," said Cat Lawrence, "now would you please follow me."

And so our friends followed Cat Lawrence in complete silence, thrilled with Zaki the Golden Lion's enormous lair. After going through several long corridors they finally found themselves in a large, spacious hall. In the center on a mound of fresh grass lay Zaki the Golden Lion.

He gazed imperiously at his visitors and roared, "So, you want to get rid of Smog Dragon do you? I have heard about this no-good Dragon and it makes me feel very good that someone has enough guts to chase him away from Crystal Lake. But it won't be an easy job."

Rainbow Captain nodded in agreement. The Lion fell to thinking. Our friends held their breath in anticipation. He continued. "When you return home, get everyone together, all the inhabitants of the lake and the forest and at sunrise when the sun's first rays fall on the lake's water, all of you will form a circle around the lake and shout this magical verse. Listen carefully."

> *Rainbow, rainbow, return to the sky;*
>
> *Chase away the Smoggy Dragon;*
>
> *Then the forest will be green;*
>
> *The water crystal clean;*
>
> *The air fresh and light;*
>
> *And the sun forever bright.*

"You must remember every word because every word is important."

"Yes, we will remember every word."

"That's not all," continued Zaki, "before you gather all the dwellers from Crystal Lake you will have to do something else."

The adventurers waited holding their breath.

"Lawrence, give him the seeds please," roared Zaki. Cat Lawrence handed Rainbow Captain a small leather bag. "This contains the magic seeds," continued Zaki the Golden Lion. "The seeds must be planted in the land of Crystal Lake. When the new trees, and the grass, and the flowers appear on the shores of Crystal Lake, and the nearby forest, and after all the dwellers of Crystal Lake have recited the magic verse in one great voice, then, and only then the terrible Smog Dragon will be destroyed. That's all," roared Zaki, "I've finished what I have to say ."

He rose to leave. Now the friends could see how truly awesome was Zaki the Golden Lion, strong and powerful in all his glory. They suddenly felt very small, and overwhelmed.

"This way please," said Cat Lawrence, leading them to the exit and waving good-bye.

"Thank you for your help Lawrence. We hope that one day you will pay us a visit at Crystal Lake."

"I doubt it. You see, I am very busy. I carry great responsibility on my shoulders," he shrugged his tiny shoulders. "But then again you never know. I may just consider visiting you on my vacation trip. Is it very cold out there where you live?"

"It gets pretty cold at times, but you can always come during the summer time," offered Miranda.

"Well then," mewed Lawrence, "I'll think about it. Thank you for inviting me. Take care of yourselves and have a good trip."

"Thank you again Lawrence," answered the friends. Rainbow Captain put the leather bag with the magic seeds into his secret pocket and they parted. In a few seconds the little group found themselves outside the Lion's quarters in the bright daylight.

*   *   *

Scratching his head with his wing, Goose Steven remembered his promise. "Now we have only to find a songbird for the lonely Cave Watcher and then we can go home." Where can we find such a bird I wonder?"

"Wait for me here," said Big White Cloud, "I'll be back soon".

The Cloud rose up and flew off. He came back shortly followed by the many-colored Calibry bird.

"Friends, this lovely songbird has volunteered* to sing for the lonely Cave Watcher. She will sing her beautiful songs for him every single morning from now on."

"Great," exclaimed Goose Steven, "Let me shake your wing dear bird." Calibry and Steven exchanged wing shakes.

"What if you get sick dear, or have to fly to some distant parts?" asked Miranda.

"Not a problem," answered the bird, "I will ask my sisters or my bird friends to replace me. Don't worry I promise on my feathers."

"It is indeed a noble* commitment*," said Rainbow Captain.

"Not at all," answered the bird. "I enjoy singing anyway and I see no reason why I can't do some singing for a lonely Cave Watcher if it makes him happy? Big White Cloud tells me that the poor thing has never been outside. Just imagine not being able to see the sun, or to smell a flower."

"Or to nibble on the fresh grass," interjected Goose Steven.

"Or not to breathe fresh air," added Miranda.

"Or not to fly high in the sky," embellished Cloud.

"You are right friends," concluded Rainbow Captain, "Maybe Cave Watcher does not need all these things, but he will be happy to know that someone cares about him. And that's enough to make anybody happy. No one should be lonely, even the creature who lives in an underground cave for a hundred years."

"Thank you very much Calibry," said Steven looking fondly at his feathered friend. "Now that I have kept my promise I feel much better and ready to go home".

"Well, if we've finished our business here we had best be on our way," and Cloud lowered himself to the ground.

They took their places on the comfortable Big White Cloud and felt themselves raised aloft.

"Good bye, Calibry," the adventurers bade farewell*.

"Good bye," sang the bird.

She watched Big White Cloud with his passengers rapidly increasing speed, rising higher and higher into the sky until the adventurers became a tiny speck, and eventually disappeared without a trace in the highest heights of the stratosphere* where even birds can never fly.

THE
..........TROUBLEDOMUS

Before them lay a long and difficult flight. They were traveling through unusually thick air and at the times it seemed like they didn't move at all. In fact Big White Cloud was moving very fast. Suddenly the winds arose and the sky grew darker. It became chilling cold, and Big White Cloud quickly descended to a lower altitude. He increased speed trying to reach a warm and safe area. Our friends clung onto Big White Cloud with all their might and Rainbow Captain held Steven and Miranda tight to himself. Big White Cloud had almost reached a bright safe area which lay ahead. However, giant, angry, clouds appeared above and beside them blocking the view, making it impossible to move forward. Big White Cloud tried to maneuver* and get away, but the giant clouds loomed larger and more furious. At that moment, terrible thunder shocked the skies and a swirling wind buffeted Big White Cloud, shredding him in half, and then everything turned dark.

A horrible noise stunned Rainbow Captain and he was torn away from Big White Cloud by an enormous force. His body was sucked into the funnel* of a twister*. A thick cold frost took his breath away, as his body tumbled through the violent waves of freezing air. He screamed but no one could hear him. The last thing he remembered was a glimpse of an empty Big White Cloud in tatters. He felt a bone shuddering blow. Then came a black silence and he no longer felt anything.

* * *

At last Rainbow Captain came to his senses and opened his eyes. He slowly moved his head and hands and lifted his legs. His body was wracked with pain. He raised to a sitting position. Sky dust covered his shoulders and clothes. He shook his head and his rainbow hair shimmered in the half light of the unfamiliar surroundings. He looked up and saw the endless dark sky with zillions of stars. Some of the stars were tiny and lonely, others were large and bright, gathered in merry-go-rounds of diverse constellations. Mysterious heavenly bodies were twinkling and shining, weaving a beautiful lace shawl for the timeless universe. Rainbow Captain thrilled to the awesome panorama of magnificent space overhead.

"Where am I?" thought Rainbow Captain, trying to recall previous events. "The seeds!" suddenly he remembered. "Oh, my magic seeds!" In agitation he patted his secret pocket. The small leather bag was inside. He cautiously took it out. "Oh thanks, thanks! My seeds are here." He sighed with relief.

"Bark, bark...," came a familiar voice from a distance.

"Miranda! Is that you? Where are you?" he screamed with joy.

"Please help me Captain, I can't move. I am stuck here."

Captain stood up and took a few steps forward. Immediately he felt some strange resistance.

He cautiously touched the air. There was a hole in the air in the place where he had put his hand. In the middle of his palm lay a gray, wet ball. "Interesting. It's like a thick fog or snow." Breaking another piece of fog he moved toward Miranda's voice. "Here you are."

Miranda happily jumped up, put her paws on Captain's shoulders and licked him on the nose.

Captain gave her a big hug.

"Are you OK?"

"I am OK. Feels strange here. Where are we and where are the others?"

"I guess they got lost during the storm," answered Rainbow Captain. "I am sure Big White Cloud will figure out something and will find us one way or another."

"I know he will. I am sure Goose Steven is with Cloud."

"Don't worry we'll be all right," answered brave Rainbow Captain, although he was not sure himself.

"I wonder what this is made of?" he said breaking a small piece out of the air.

"I noticed it too. Look!" Miranda wagged her tail creating different shapes in the thick air.

Suddenly they saw a crowd of strange creatures who were heading toward them. Miranda pricked her ears and came closer to the Captain. The creatures were breaking a path in the strange substance leaving behind a long tunnel. They were dressed in long black capes. Their heads were square shaped and they produced strange chirping noises. They had a most unusual feature: their feet were pointed backwards. Scuttling up to the Rainbow Captain and Miranda, they surrounded them in a tight circle. They were heavily armed and each of them had a stick, which they used to clear the way through the thick substance.

"Freeze," ordered the leader. As he spoke a red flash went on on his computer like head.

"Who are you?" asked Rainbow Captain stepping back. Miranda clenched to Captain's leg.

Captain gently patted her on the back. He felt the tension of her body.

"Who are we?" The creature started laughing and the rest of the group joined him. The lights on their heads lit up and a weird metallic chattering burst forth.

"How about who are YOU and most important, how did you get here? This is a restricted area of the cosmos and one must have a special permit to visit our planet," said the leader angrily.

"I won't answer your questions until you introduce yourself and tell me what forces you represent," answered Rainbow Captain fearlessly. Miranda waggled her tail in support.

"Very well. Then listen carefully stranger. We are a space clan called Trabikuses and I am Greatest Trabikus, Master of the Universe."

"I am not so sure about that," Captain thought to himself but said nothing.

Greatest Trabikus continued: "I am also the Chief Commander of the strongest army in this galaxy* and these are my officers." He pointed at the group behind them.

"Yeaaah," cried the officers in approval.

"And what is the name of your wonderful planet and this thick substance we are trying to walk through?" politely inquired Miranda.

"Our planet is called Troubledomus and the substance is called the Tuman Ring. It's a security ring which encircles our secret Operation Zone. Whoever breaches the Tuman Ring should be prepared to face deadly consequences. He raised his stick and pointed it at Miranda. This is a tumancracker. It has many purposes and one of them is to strike unwanted intruders. Who are you to ask anyway? No one is allowed to speak without my permission." He kicked Miranda in the chest. Miranda yelped.

"Easy," said Captain stepping forward, "We don't know your rules."

"I'll make sure you'll learn them fast," screamed Greatest Trabikus striking Rainbow Captain in the face. Captain shook his head and his rainbow hair produced a sharp flash of bright light which blocked the blow.

"Never hit me or my Dog again, for I am also a space creature," he said with dignity*.

"We'll see about that. Deliver information!" ordered angry Greatest Trabikus turning to his subordinate*. There was a noise at the officer's head as it flashed with a yellow light and he chirped something in a most strange language resembling neither human nor animal, nor any other sound that the adventurers had ever heard.

"Kur, kun, gor grn, rraklnm...," continued Information Officer. Greatest Trabikus translated:

"Names: Rainbow Captain and Miranda the Dog.

Planet: Tiny Planet beside the rainbow and planet Earth.

Place of residence: Crystal Lake.

Hobbies: Cleaning the sky and caring for the environment*.

Additional information and secret file deliver at once," he ordered again.

One more time the computer head went through his noisy, weird routine. It went on for a while without giving any results.

"Enough! All I asked for was just a piece of information and you are giving me a headache instead. What on earth is wrong with you, officer?" yelled Greatest Trabikus in frustration.

"Excuse me," interjected Miranda, recovering from her pain, "but you are not on Earth Mr. Greatest Trabikus."

"Shut up, dog. No one asked your opinion. It's just a saying which I heard from my prisoners from your stupid planet."

"Earth is not a stupid planet. On the contrary it is quite beautiful. I can assure you, " said Rainbow Captain.

"What! Who gave you the right to speak in my presence?" Greatest Trabikus screamed rudely. "You can only answer my questions and obey my orders."

"Well, that's a matter of opinion, sir," said Rainbow Captain trying to be polite despite shaking with a rage unknown to him.

"That's it! I've had enough of you and your dog. You are under arrest for entering my territory without permission and for arguing with me. Off to jail with them!" ordered Greatest Trabikus.

At that very moment, something fell from above drilling a hole through the Tuman and landing on Captain's shoulder. It moved, opened its eyes, and only then Captain noticed the familiar bow tie.

"Steven! It's Steven," exclaimed Captain and Miranda together.

Although poor Goose Steven was in total shock, he recognized his dear friends immediately and smiled weakly. "It seems to me I have been flying forever and ever. Where are we friends?" he groaned.

Abruptly, a tiny object fell down through the same hole made by Steven and landed on the ground in front of Miranda.

"Here is you hat, Steven," said Miranda.

Rainbow Captain gently put Steven down. Steven picked up his hat, shook off the sky dust and placed it firmly on his head.

"In answer to your question, friend, we are sort of visiting Troubledomus planet. This is Greatest Trabikus and his officers," explained Rainbow Captain .

Greatest Trabikus and the officers were also recovering from the shock caused by Steven's sudden arrival. Some of them looked up fearing more surprises.

"Who is this now?" inquired Greatest Trabikus pointing at Steven. "Information at once," he ordered.The Information officer began his search.

"So, you are Goose Steven from planet Earth. You also live at Crystal Lake. Your hobbies are nibbling green grass, swimming in the water and flying in the sky. Identifying characteristic is the bow tie. What is the bow tie for? Does it contain a secret electronic device?" pressed Greatest Trabikus. Steven didn't answer. Still in shock he simply stared at Greatest Trabikus.

"I assure you sir, it does not contain any electronic device. I believe it is a matter of personal taste, sir. You like wearing guns and a tumancracker and he likes his bow tie," Rainbow Captain said trying to help.

"That tells me nothing. I accuse you of spying for enemy forces. You're under arrest," screamed Greatest Trabikus. "Cuff them and take them to jail."

The officers cuffed Rainbow Captain and chained Steven's tiny leg to Miranda's. The friends started pushing their way through the thick Tuman towards the unknown.

*   *   *

As soon as they began walking they understood the reason for the Trabikuses' weird backward feet. Passage over Troubledomus ground was laborious because of the volcanic rocks and mud under foot and the almost impenetrable Tuman Ring. Trabikuses appeared to have less trouble. Their backward feet didn't trip them up and with their powerful tumancrackers they blasted their way through. After many stumbles and tumbles and constant prodding by the officers, the trip through the Tuman Ring was finally over. They came out of it exhausted and thirsty.

The first thing that caught their eyes was an awesome construction. Situated on top of a hill was multistory space ship. The ship was surrounded by a fence with a huge gate. They were heading toward the gate. Goose Steven couldn't walk any longer and Miranda pulled him gently up the hill. They approached the immense gate which was made from a strange stone and materials unknown to them.

The group stopped and the friends could rest for the first time since they started the dreadful journey through the Tuman Ring. Greatest Trabikus touched the wall with his tumancracker and the square head of a duty officer appeared on a small screen. The duty officer stared fearfully up at Greatest Trabikus and the gate slowly slid up without a sound.

"We have arrived at the Operation Zone," said Greatest Trabikus motioning them through the gate with his tumancracker. "You won't feel yourselves at home here," he said with a wicked grin.

The gate crashed down behind them.

...............IMPRISONMENT

The Operation Zone was a very busy place. In the middle of it stood a spaceship surrounded by a variety of construction activities and space vehicles. There was a tall telescope tower which monitored every movement inside the Operation Zone and the space above and around it. Periodically the screen showed the whole of Troubledomus with its Tuman Ring and cosmic space beyond the planet. Inside, the ship consisted of many stories linked by stairs. Elevators moved up and down and there was an assembly line on each floor.

The friends were now moving toward one of the elevators. They could see strange creatures working at the assembly line under the supervision of Trabikus guards. Some of the workers resembled human beings, others were of origins unknown to the adventurers.

All at once there was a commotion. The friends attention was drawn to a Green Creature with a large head and a very short arms who could not work as quickly as the others. He was taken aside and the Trabikus guard shouted at him, pushing him on the floor. The Green Creature yelled in horror and then fell silent. He was carried off and thrown into a recycling bin used for disposal of those who could no longer work. A puff of green smoke signaled the end of the Green Creature. The adventurers watched in terror the whole ordeal.

"Where are they taking us?" trembled Miranda.

"Be quiet. Watch the way and try to remember every nook and cranny," Rainbow Captain whispered.

Suddenly Goose Steven, exhausted, collapsed on the floor. One of the Trabikuses approached him and raised his stick.

"Sir," pleaded Rainbow Captain anxiously to Greatest Trabikus, "please allow me to carry my bird."

"I need the bird for the interrogation. He will be more useful alive so you may carry your bird stranger. Uncuff them," he ordered one of the officers.

"No one escapes Operation Zone alive anyway," he chuckled. They were uncuffed.

"I am grateful sir," said Rainbow Captain. He gently picked up Goose Steven and they continued their trip through the ship.

They stopped near the elevator. It came down and one of the Trabikuses pushed Rainbow Captain and Miranda inside. The door closed behind them and the elevator rapidly descended.

When it stopped, the door opened and they were vacuumed into a black tube connected to the elevator. They were whirling through the dark spiral tunnel with increasing speed. The rushing air propelled their bodies forward.

"Don't fight it," screamed Captain to his friends. "Just let it move you along or it will break your bones."

Miranda and Steven relaxed their bodies and let the crazy force carry them through the tunnel. Finally the weird trip was over and they fell onto a hard surface. Steven's hat and Captain's boot plopped down beside them.

They sat in the darkness gathering their wits. Miranda shook her head.

"I am still dizzy," she said smelling the air around her.

"Take a deep breath and it will go away. And how are you Steven?" asked Rainbow Captain. "I am OK. I am getting used to these crazy flights. Remember, I am a Goose not a chicken. I am a flying bird after all."

"You are indeed," said Rainbow Captain.

"What should we do next?" asked Miranda.

"I am sure we'll find out soon," replied Captain and before he finished speaking they heard an awful clanging noise. The wall in front of them moved up and they were blinded by a flash light.

"Get up!" they heard an abrupt command. "Follow me." They jumped to their feet and followed Gigantic Trabikus Guard. He was so huge that his broad shoulders blocked the view in front of them. They stepped into some slimy substance and their trip became increasingly difficult. Gigantic Trabikus Guard in the meantime was speeding full steam ahead, his huge backward feet sliding easily along the messy path.

"It's almost like walking inside a pencil box half full of cooked porridge," said Rainbow Captain.

"This part will be easy to remember," noted Miranda as she struggled forward.

"No talking," screamed Gigantic Trabikus Guard. He tried to strike Rainbow Captain with the tumancracker but Captain shook his head and his hair again produced a punch of multicolored light and stopped the stick.

"Hey, how did you do that?" asked Gigantic Trabikus Guard amazed.

"I am a space creature like you are. I have my powers."

"I feel sorry for you boy. Greatest Trabikus doesn't like strangers. He thinks they're all spies. He exterminates them. He even exterminated my best friend from nearby Orus planet who came just for a visit." That story sent chills through the adventurers spines.

"Why did he do that?"

"Because Greatest Trabikus is constantly fighting Orus. He wants to conquer Orus and to rule it. But so far he keeps losing the wars. Despite that Greatest Trabikus' forces are very strong, Oruses are super intelligent creatures and hard to beat."

"Sir," asked Goose Steven," Why don't you help us to escape? We are innocent like your friend was."

"No one escapes from Troubledomus, bird," Gigantic Trabikus Guard said after a long pause.

"In any event ," said Miranda politely, "thank you for talking to us."

They continued the rest of the trip in silence. The tunnel came to an end and they found themselves standing on a transparent panel. It began to move upward. Underneath they saw small cells filled with prisoners who were lying on the floor exhausted after a hard working day. The panel reached the top level and stopped. The wall in front of them was raised and they walked inside the cell. The wall slid down again separating them from Gigantic Trabikus Guard who disappeared below. Shortly, two new officers entered the cell. They looked the same except that one of them had a purple cape instead of the usual black.

"I am from Execution Unit," the officer in purple announced. The other Trabikus pointed a short laser pistol at the travelers. The Trabikus in purple patted Rainbow Captain down for weapons with lizard quick movements. He found the secret pocket, unzipped it and took out the leather bag with the magic seeds.

"What are these?" he demanded. Rainbow Captain felt sick to his stomach.

"Nothing important, sir...."

"You are to call me Master One!" he interrupted Rainbow Captain.

"Nothing important Master One," repeated Captain, "these are just some seeds we are hoping to plant at our home at Crystal Lake."

"Who said you are going home. No one ever returned home from Troubledomus."

He handed the bag of seeds to the second officer who stuck it into a pouch on his belt.

"You," he pointed at Miranda, "are coming with me." He seemed not to notice Goose Steven at all.

"Where are you taking her Master One?" asked Captain.

Master One didn't answer. He drilled Rainbow Captain with the cold empty holes which served for eyes and raised his tumancracker.

"Be brave," said Rainbow Captain to his dear friend.

Miranda wagged her tail good-bye and sadly followed Master One and his officer outside the cell. Rainbow Captain and Goose Steven sank to the floor. It was hard and cold as ice.

"What are we going to do?" asked Goose Steven.

"I don't know," said Rainbow Captain. "We must think of something. Think hard Steven."

*   *   *

Goose Steven didn't sleep that night. All night he was scratching the nape of his neck. (If you remember, my friend, this is the way he got his brilliant ideas.)

Early in the morning Steven shook Rainbow Captain who was still asleep.

"Wake up Captain, wake up."

Rainbow Captain opened his eyes and jumped to his feet. "What's happening?"

"Well, you told me to think hard and I thought all night. And this is what we can do. We will tell Greatest Trabikus the whole truth and we'll ask him to let us go home."

"What about Miranda? We must find Miranda."

"I don't know how to find Miranda," said Steven almost in tears for he missed Miranda terribly and worried about her.

"It may work," said Rainbow Captain.

The front wall slid up and a strange creature entered the cell. He had long gray hair and a messy beard. His feet faced frontwards they noticed. He carried a small black box and tumancracker.

"Breakfast time," he said opening a black box and placing it on the floor.

There the prisoners found some kind of yellow liquid and a rusty-colored, soapy-looking item.

"Eat it. It has some vitamins," said the creature pointing at the soap. "The liquid too. It's good for you."

Rainbow Captain picked up the soapy thing and broke off a small hunk which he carefully put in his mouth. "It tastes awful," he said with a grimace. "Do we have to eat this?"

"Well, that's all the food you get today, my friend."

"You know," said Rainbow Captain smiling, "you are the first person who called me friend since we landed in Troubledomus. Who are you?"

"I think I am a human. I have to use a washroom occasionally. Trabikuses don't use washrooms as you probably know."

"We didn't know that, but carry on, please."

"I can't tell you very much about myself only that Greatest Trabikus destroyed my spaceship and took me prisoner."

"Do you know your name?" asked Goose Steven.

"Not really. They did something to my head and I lost my memory. Here they call me Beetikus."

"What do you do here?"

"I am a cleaning person. Here is my broom." He lifted his tumancracker and pushed a small button. It made slight noise and turned into a sort of vacuum cleaner.

"Neat," exclaimed Captain.

78

"Shhh! Please be quiet," warned Beetikus. "Never indicate that you're happy or interested in something otherwise they exterminate you."

"Did you see a dog here anywhere by chance?" asked Steven.

"A dog? What is it? Sounds familiar."

"A dog, you know. She barks and she smells things." Rainbow Captain jumped down onto all fours, barked and ran around Goose Steven smelling him vigorously.

"Oh," whispered Beetikus opening wide his eyes and covering his mouth with the palm of his hand. "It's an animal isn't it? I think I had a dog when I was a child." His sad gray eyes lit up for a second. "You know what, I saw a dog! I gave her some food. She is in one of the cells below."

"Did you hear that Steven? It must be our Miranda. Please take good care of her," pleaded Rainbow Captain.

"I'll see what I can do." He started vacuuming the cell.

"Listen friend, could you take us to Miranda and help us to escape. We must escape."

"You must be joking. No one ever escaped Troubledomus."

He silently disappeared through the exit wall. They ate the rest of their breakfasts, cleaning up every drop of the vile liquid.

"Yaack," said Rainbow Captain.

"Gross," agreed Goose Steven.

"Everyone must have breakfast Steven, even a prisoner."

"I know. But this kind of breakfast gives me goose bumps."

"It's because you're a Goose."

"You may be right," agreed Steven.

*   *   *

They heard heavy steps and a clinking noise. Master One and his subordinate* ordered them out. They escorted them to a different cell with a huge screen on the ceiling. The temperature in the cell was changing wildly from chilling cold to burning heat. The lights constantly switched from impossibly sun bright to the black darkness with flashing blood-red shadows on the walls and ceiling. The floor was spinning under their feet and they were holding tightly to each other trying to maintain their balance. Horrible screams and grisly sounds dominated everything in the cell.

This scary reception went on for some time and then the racket abruptly stopped. The floor gradually steadied and the chaotic light settled to a deep purple color. The two friends recoiled in horror at the sight of a recycling bin in the corner, similar to the one in which the unfortunate Green Creature with the short hands had lost his life. The bones of some unrecognizable space creatures were scattered all over the cell.

The prisoners were pushed in the middle. Then the screen over their heads lit up and they saw Greatest Trabikus's image.

"Accused are ready for interrogation Your Greatness," announced Master One who seemed to appear from nowhere.

"Very well. Have they been tortured yet?" demanded Greatest Trabikus.

80

"Not, yet Your Greatness. We figured that they will not be able to withstand the torture due to their small size. They are the smallest prisoners we've ever had in Troubledomus. Our torture unit is not designed for such puny species. There would be nothing left of them after the torture. However, if you wish we will deposit them into the torture unit right away."

"Hmm. We'll have to put it off for now. It's a shame though. The torture unit must be redesigned immediately," ordered Greatest Trabikus.

"Yes Your Greatness, the torture unit will be redesigned immediately," repeated Master One.

"Proceed then with the interrogation."

"Proceed," repeated Master One swatting Rainbow Captain hard on the back with his tumancracker.

"What do you want me to do?"

"Explain how you got to Troubledomus. Who sent you here and who are you spying for?" demanded Greatest Trabikus. Rainbow Captain hesitated trying to gather his thoughts.

"Proceed," Master One whacked him again.

"If you continue hitting me I will forget everything," said brave Rainbow Captain.

"Speak now or you will be exterminated," ordered Greatest Trabikus.

"We are not spies or anything like that," Rainbow Captain started slowly, "we were traveling back home from our mission and got into a terrible storm which landed us on your planet."

"What kind of mission and why do you carry on such activities?"

"Well, we just...," hesitated Captain, "we must destroy Smog Dragon who makes life impossible at Crystal Lake. Don't we Steven?"

"Yeaaa," shouted small Steven with all his might flapping his wings up in the air, "we must destroy this no-good Dragon."

Master One who was guarding the prisoners moved back slightly placing his hand on his gun.

"How come I never heard of this Smog Dragon?" asked Greatest Trabikus observing the prisoners with cold curiosity.

"Perhaps your information officers' systems are dated and need to be changed," Captain answered quickly.

"Possible. Lately they make more noise than communications. I shall destroy them and replace them with a more advanced system."

"That would certainly solve the problem with your communications system all right, Your Greatness," Rainbow Captain concurred enthusiastically. "Also, as I am sure you are aware, these are just computerized units. If something undetected goes wrong, then everything falls apart," he continued knowingly.

"I am aware of that. How do I know that you're are telling the truth about yourselves?" asked Greatest Trabikus somewhat puzzled.

"Well, if it wouldn't be for a storm we would never end up on your planet. As you and your officers noticed we don't have any space craft or any other means to move through space. Our friend Big White Cloud was our sky transportation."

"Hm...where is he now?"

"We don't know. He was lost during the storm and we are very concerned for his safety. Now, don't you think we are telling the truth?"

"I don't think," answered Greatest Trabikus, "I observe, I sense, I calculate and I make decisions. And with you I sense that the probability of you telling the truth is fifty percent, so I've decided to give you a chance but not before you experience our torture unit. If you survive the torture I will consider keeping you alive as my workers on the Assembly Line."

"May I ask for my seeds back Your Greatness?"

"What do you need seeds for?"

"See, Your Greatness," answered Rainbow Captain his brain working fast "mhh... it's our food. It's the only one thing we can eat. We are not accustomed to your rations and we need to gain all the strength we can to survive the torture. The only way to do it is to consume our own food sir."

"Mmm, yummy," suddenly interjected Goose Steven. He jumped patting himself on the belly, his long neck sticking out and he shouted like only geese can do:

> *We will eat our seeds*
>
> *And we'll feel like mighty beasts*
>
> *We'll become the strongest creatures*
>
> *And survive all sorts of tortures*

Master One stepped forward and aimed his laser pistol at the prisoners. Greatest Trabikus glared at Steven.

"Forgive him Your Greatness, he always goes crazy when he hears about the seeds. It makes him strong" said Captain sending Steven an approving glance.

After a long pause Greatest Trabikus said, "Normally you both would be executed but I have something better for you. Who brings them their food?"

"A creature commonly known as Beetikus, Your Greatness," answered Master One.

"Very well. They will be fed their seeds for breakfast. After that they will be deposited into the torture unit for three cycles and then I'll make the final decision."

"Yes, Your Greatness."

"You better eat enough of your food for tomorrow, strangers as you'll need all the strength you have." With this Greatest Trabikus disappeared from the screen.

Rainbow Captain and Goose Steven couldn't believe their luck. They were escorted back to their cell where they were left alone.

"How did you come up with such a story so fast?" Steven blurted out.

"Because we thought about it together, remember? One head is good but two even better. You did quite a job yourself."

"I did?"

"Oh yes. You surprised the wits out of them. How did you come up with the song?"

"I don't know. I thought you could use some support," answered Steven

"You were right. I think your song did the trick. Together we looked very convincing," said Rainbow Captain with a big smile. "Anyway, there is nothing we can do till Beetikus comes in the early morning. Let's have a nap in the meantime."

WAR

............AND ESCAPE

They slept. Goose Steven dreamed about flying over Crystal Lake and landing into tall juicy green grass. Rainbow Captain in his dream saw Big White Cloud and heard his airy resonant voice." Don't worry friend, I'll be there for you."

Captain opened his eyes and stretched. The entrance wall came up, Beetikus entered the cell. He was wearing a purple cape. Something was moving and breathing under it. It came out and in the darkness of the cell Captain recognized Miranda. She put her paws on Captain's shoulders and he gave her a big hug. He almost cried with happiness. Then Miranda came to Steven and gently licked him on the beak waking him up. "Miranda, it's you! You came back."

"Please be quiet," warned Beetikus, "we'll die a horrible death if they hear us. Here are your seeds. I understand it's your essential food."

"It's more than food friend. May be sometime we can tell you the whole story."

Rainbow Captain took the small leather bag and hid it deep into his secret pocket.

"Thank you Beetikus for bringing Miranda to us. You're the bravest creature in space."

"That was nothing. She just slipped under my cape and we walked together like one person."

"We don't need to tell you what we would like to do next," Captain said in a whisper.

"No, you don't," Beetikus replied, "I'll help you to escape. Follow me until we reach the Control Section. You need to find the secret code for the exit file in the main system in order to get outside the ship. Any space vehicle will get you out of the Operation Zone through the Tuman Ring and toward the edge of Troubledomus. I wish you luck."

"What about the guards?".

"In this part of the ship they're using the Watching Element. It's like an invisible camera located almost everywhere. It monitors every move and reports to the Headquarters of Operation Zone. You have to move very fast. You have to be ahead of the report."

"It's quite difficult I assume."

"It's almost impossible."

"Come with us Beetikus."

"No, I belong here."

"You don't belong here. You belong on Earth."

"What if I become a useless creature and everyone will hate me on Earth. What if I am not going to like it there? Besides there is no guarantee you'll manage to escape yourself. What if Trabikuses catch you and throw you in a torturing unit?"

"They are going to do it anyway, so we may as well take our chances. Come with us."

"No, it's too risky. I am staying here."

"What if they find out that you helped us?"

"I'll be the last one they would suspect. Now, let's go before I change my mind."

They followed Beetikus through the long empty corridors of the spaceship.

"Listen," whispered Miranda. They heard the distant chirping of Trabikuses.

"We can't go back. Get under my cape fast," said Beetikus.

They did just that. Beetikus got his tumancracker and pretended that he was cleaning the floor. Under his cape, like in a slow dance, the friends followed his every movement.

The group of Trabikuses approached them.

"What are you doing here at this early hour, creature?"

"I am following Greatest Trabikus's instructions. He is expecting an important space delegation in the morning and I am ordered to make everything spotless. For this purpose I was given this new cape so I can be easily recognized and move freely through the ship. No one is allowed to interrupt my work. Greatest Trabikus will exterminate me and those who make me lose precious time," said Beetikus in his calm quiet voice. Frozen with fear the friends held their breath.

"Leave him alone," said Master One and they continued marching in the opposite direction.

For a while Beetikus pretended to work. When Trabikuses disappeared from view, they hurried along the dangerous passage, Beetikus pausing to sweep here and there, until they reached the Control Section.

"Here you are. I wish you luck."

"Thank you Beetikus, we'll never forget you."

They entered a spacious round hall with a large complicated computer system whirring and flashing. Rainbow Captain studied the system carefully. He managed to open it and to get into the depths of cosmic cyber space. First of all he located the security report from Watching Element which traced their trip with Beetikus from their cell. He erased it just before the send command appeared.

"Now they won't get this report. They'll think we are still in our cells."

He was now trying to find a secret matching code which would enable them to exit the ship. He pushed different numbers and sets of keys, trying to find the right combination. He went on for a long time without result.

"I am not familiar with this system."

"We better get going soon," said Miranda "I sense something is happening."

"Here," exclaimed Rainbow Captain "I found it." The computer screen produced a musical sound and they could see the emergency exit map with full instructions. "There, now I know how to get out from here. We have to find a small door at the end of the old section of the ship. It will take us to the elevators, from where we can reach the exit easily."

Suddenly a powerful explosion shook the ship violently. Sirens shrieked. They heard Trabikuses approaching the Control Room. The fierce turbulence and banging continued.

A loud speaker shrilled above the racket.

"Attention all troops and systems. We are now in a state of War with planet Orus. To your positions everyone," roared Greatest Trabikus.

"Run friends, run for our lives."

They rushed out and almost immediately heard a shout.

"Freeze!"

"Get on my back Steven," screamed Miranda.

"If only I could fly," Steven cried.

"You will soon."

"Speed up you guys!" yelled Rainbow Captain.

Trabikuses were in hot pursuit, sparks flying from their backwards feet. The friends spotted a small, almost invisible door.

"This must be it. Through here! "

They flew through the door which immediately slammed behind them. They found themselves in an abandoned part of the ship and they climbed a set of stairs and came to the elevator.

Suddenly Gigantic Trabikus Guard appeared in front of them.

"It's you again. What are you doing here?"

"Please, let us continue."

"I am not suppose to do it," he said.

"They killed your friend remember? And they'll kill us too," reminded Miranda.

"All right. Go."

They jumped into the elevator and it took them down below.

"I remember this place," said Miranda.

"Don't tell me we'll have to fly through the swirling tube again."

"It's better than a torture unit Steven."

"It will take us outside the ship into the Operation Zone," said Gigantic Trabikus. "Follow me."

"Did you join Orus's forces ?" guessed Rainbow Captain.

"How did you know?"

"You're different from other Trabikuses."

"You may as well know the truth. Greatest Trabikus wants to destroy every planet around Troubledomus. He then wants to move into different galaxies and destroy them as well.

Eventually he wants to rule all the cosmos. You probably noticed an assembly line where all the prisoners were working. They are making special devices which will be used to devastate the environment* of the various planets and it's life, except for a few creatures who will be later enslaved by the Greatest Trabikus. He will go there with his troops and set up his way of existence."

"Is this why he calls himself Master of the Universe?"

"Yes."

"There is no such a thing as one master of the Universe. Each of us has equal rights. And each one has the right to live in a free and peaceful environment*," said Rainbow Captain.

"You are right. Orus also believes in freedom of every creature on every planet. This is why I joined his forces. We don't want Trabikuses to become our masters."

The ship was rocked again by another enormous explosion. They were thrown forward through a hole which was blasted through the wall of the ship and found themselves outside in the Operation Zone. The fight was on.

They ran to one of the space vehicles and hopped inside as Trabikuses counterattacked Oruses' small ships with crisscrossing fire. Blinding balls of multicolored flame lit up the cosmos and thunderous blasts that shook Troubledomus planet to the core issued from the deadly Trabikus weapons.

In response a massive ship descended from outer space and a platoon of Orus fighters jumped to the ground. They launched a formidable attack against the Trabikus stronghold. The immense, indestructible ship served as a vehicle and a weapon at the same time. With the last series of precision blasts, the Operation Zone was destroyed and the remains of Greatest Trabikus's force fell to the red hot ground. Trabikuses crumpled and twisted where they fell, melting into small pools of toxic liquid.

"That was the shortest war I ever heard of," said Rainbow Captain peering out from the safety of the space ship.

"What?"

"Can't you hear me?"

"I can't hear you," said a stunned Steven.

"What are you saying. I can't hear you," said Miranda. They shook their heads violently.

"That's better. Can you hear me now?"

At that moment they were approached by Orus himself accompanied by Gigantic Trabikus Guard.

"Here are the creatures I told you about," said Gigantic Trabikus pointing at the small group.

"Congratulations. You are free now," said Orus.

"We need some transportation to go back. Can you help us with it?"

Orus pointed to a small rocket. "Use one of our landing crafts. Follow the path through the Tuman Ring. It will take you to the edge of Troubledomus. Someone is waiting for you there."

"Whoever could it be?"

"Get down there fast and you'll find out."

"Thank you for everything Orus. Good by Giant Trabikus."

They boarded the rocket and it soared aloft. Following its computer's instructions they flew over the remains of Operation Zone and along the pathway through the Tuman. In no time the rocket brought them to the edge of Troubledomus. They descended to the ground and looked around. Nothing! No one to greet them. Just silence and the vastness of space hanging over their heads.

"This is exactly the place where we landed after the storm," said Rainbow Captain.

"I remember this place too," said Miranda.

"Well, then you must remember me my friends," they heard a familiar airy voice.

"Cloud!" yelled Goose Steven.

"It's our Cloud! Where are you?" shouted Captain and Miranda.

"Look that must be him," exclaimed Rainbow Captain pointing at the purplish-blue mass of soft air coming towards them.

Big White Cloud descended in front of the adventurers.

"Oh, Cloud, dear Cloud! How did you find us?"

"Hello dear friends. I have been looking for you everywhere. I remembered the point where the storm that tore us away from each other took place. So as soon as I had regained my strength I began searching for you around Troubledomus. I then learned from the space informants about your imprisonment and the War between Greatest Trabikus and Orus. I knew you wouldn't miss a chance to escape. I sent a message to Oruses through the space informants and I asked them to help you."

"They were indeed helpful. They provided us with this small rocket and here we are. Am I ever happy to see you alive." "We are also very happy to see you dear Cloud."

"You changed your color," noted Rainbow Captain.

"I had to. There is certainly no place for white clouds to hide in this place."

"And look at your scars," exclaimed Miranda.

"How did you heal yourself after the terrible storm?" asked Rainbow Captain hugging his dear friend.

"Well, I collected some of my pieces after the storm and I used the Tuman to patch my wounds. Then I rolled in space dust and rushed as high up into space as I could. There I stayed in hiding until I was strong enough to fly again and now I am even stronger than before the storm, although I may look a little smaller."

"Don't worry about your size. We'll fatten you up as soon as we reach Earth," said Rainbow Captain lovingly. "The most important thing is that you are back with us," said Goose Steven.

"And we will never lose you again," added Miranda.

"So friends, are we ready to go back home to Crystal Lake?"

"Yes we are."

"Then off we go."

And so the happy adventurers seated themselves comfortably and at full speed headed back home, away from Troubledomus toward Earth and their beloved Crystal Lake.

............BACK HOME

In the meantime the situation at Crystal Lake had much worsened. The once splendid green grass had turned into dirty clumps. The water in the lake had darkened and was choked with underwater vegetation. The inhabitants of the underwater world had hidden wherever they could. The magical Crystal Lake had been transformed into a dismal, neglected bog ruled over by the repulsive Smog Dragon. Our friends hastened as fast as they could. Strong winds pushed Big White Cloud who was flying at top speed, easily following the now familiar route.

On the way back they met a flock of wild geese flying south who slowed down to speak with the unusual group of adventurers. Never before had they met a cloud in the sky filled with passengers.

"Hello there," squawked the geese, "who are you and where are you going?"

"We are returning home to Crystal Lake to chase away Smog Dragon?"

"How are you going to do that? He's scared away every living creature and destroyed the environment for miles around," said the leader.

"We flew around the world in search of a magic potion and we found it," explained Rainbow Captain. "Now we need all the help we can get. Would you like to help us?"

"Sure thing," squawked the geese, "we want to help. We hate the dirty monster."

"Then fly with us to Crystal Lake," called Goose Steven.

Suddenly he spread his wings, took a deep breath, flapped his wings furiously and shot out of his boots into the air leaving behind astonished Big White Cloud, Rainbow Captain and Miranda.

" Follow me, brothers, and don't fall behind!"

The flock turned and followed Goose Steven. He now was ahead of everyone and the wild geese were hard pressed to keep up with him.

"Hey friends," called Steven with joy, "there is nothing better than flying on your own."

As they flew along, Steven recounted their adventures over the ocean, in the jungle and on Troubledomus. He mentioned to the wild geese angry Python and Pink Flamingo who had run away and left them alone to fight Python. He told them about polluted cities, bald spots in the jungle and oil spills in the ocean. He also told them about poor Beetikus who could never make up his mind and of the terrible, destructive Trabikuses.

Miranda overheard Steven's story and said, "That's true. The journey at times was difficult but we met many fine animals and creatures. Do you remember old Bald Eagle on the cliff who told us the route to follow and the monkey who defended you against Dreaded Python? And don't forget about Merry Dolphin. If it weren't for him, Trout Gordon would probably have died in the fish bowl".

"But I still don't understand why Beetikus didn't escape with us?"

"Trabikuses made him insecure by destroying his confidence. But they didn't kill it entirely. He helped us escape from Troubledomus, remember."

"I hope he will get back his confidence somehow. I got mine and now I can fly again," said Goose Steven happily.

Big White Cloud coasted along beside Steven and the wild geese who attentively listened to the whole conversation. The sky was blue and peaceful, the winds were warm and strong and the whole company took great pleasure in their purposeful journey.

"I think," remarked Rainbow Captain, "that there are many more good creatures in the world than evil ones. Surely, if all the good were to band together they would win over the bad."

"I think you are right friend. I have flown around the world and I know what you're talking about."

They were now passing over the ocean and Big White Cloud descended to a lower altitude where the winds were even warmer. Goose Steven took off higher into the sky followed by the wild geese flock.

"We'll see you at Crystal Lake Steven. I'm going to check up on our ocean friends," puffed Cloud.

"See you soon."

As they flew over the ocean Merry Dolphin and Trout Gordon came to greet them.

"Hi there!" cried Gordon and Merry Dolphin who were very happy to see their friends again.

"Did you manage to find the magic potion?" asked Gordon.

"Yes we found the magic potion and we hope you'll make it home soon."

"You bet. I love the ocean and my new friends but I do miss my home. See you at Crystal Lake," answered the exuberant Gordon.

"Good luck to you on your mission," Merry Dolphin wished them and they both began a happy sea dance to celebrate the return of their friends.

*　*　*

And so after thousands and thousands of miles, countless countries and cities, lakes, seas, mountains and forests lay behind them, our friends finally arrived back home at their beloved Crystal Lake. Big White Cloud landed on the ravaged lake shore and our adventurers stepped onto the ground. Goose Steven and the flock of wild geese had arrived earlier and had settled nearby.

"Look how dirty the water is in the lake! And there is no grass, no flowers", blurted some wild geese.

Silence had descended over the lake except for the snoring of Smog Dragon. Then, coming from somewhere hidden within the forest a small hare showed up.

"The grass does not grow here any longer, neither do flowers. Everything has been poisoned by Smog Dragon."

A lonely beaver sat on the shore of the lake observing the remains of his home destroyed by pollution.

"As you can see, we are the last ones here. We have no place to go, no place to hide," he said with great sadness.

"Would you like to help us to destroy the monster?" asked Rainbow Captain.

"Would I ever? But I can see no way to help?" he looked around dejectedly.

"Wait," said Miranda," This place is in bad shape, indeed, but you can help. Stay with us."

"Listen all of you and you will find out how," said Rainbow Captain. "Friends, do you remember what Zaki told us to do? We must gather together absolutely all of the inhabitants of Crystal Lake and the forest dwellers. We must be quick and quiet. We must not wake up the monster. If he suspects something we will be in deep trouble." He looked at Miranda. "You have the most difficult task. You are going to be our watchdog. You must watch over Smog Dragon. Goose Steven, you'll stay on the lake shore and when the animals begin to gather here, you must teach them the words to the magic verse. Remember, absolutely everybody must know the verse's words. You geese fly as far as you can and find all the forest and lake creatures. Tell them we need them all here to fight Smog Dragon. Everything must be ready by sunrise."

Rainbow Captain straddled Big White Cloud and they rose into the sky. He got the leather bag out and commenced scattering magic seeds in all directions while Cloud was spinning in circles over Crystal Lake and the ancient forest. From the air they could see Miranda. She was scampering toward Smog Dragon's lair. When she was halfway there, she stopped and crept off to one side. Although she was a very brave dog, she felt a little bit frightened.

From close up, Smog Dragon looked even more terrifying. Piles of stinking garbage were stuck to his long tail and reeking black smoke billowed from his mouth. It was impossible to breathe near the monster.

Miranda was almost choking.

She crept cautiously toward the Dragon after nightfall and silently began her watch. As dawn approached she could see the Dragon even more clearly.

He was the ugliest, scariest thing she had ever seen in her life and she had to force herself not to run away.

Rainbow Captain had saved a handful of seeds from last night's work which he now threw over Dragon's head. One seed stuck in his empty eye, another in his smoky chimney and still another in his long destructive tail.

The seeds started magically growing, turning into green sprouts. They grew faster and faster changing into beautiful trees, tall grass and flowers. The water in Crystal Lake also became clean and returned to it's natural sparkle.

Rainbow Captain could see how fish were rising from the bottom of the lake towards the shining surface which grew light as dawn approached.

You may recall my friend, that the magical words must be chanted at sunrise. Our friends' efforts were not in vain, and the animals had already begun to gather on the shore of the lake just before dawn. Rabbits, hedgehogs and foxes with all their little ones ran to meet Goose Steven. From far away where the wild geese had been searching, a proud deer could be seen leaping toward the shore.

They were joined by a gray wolf who had decided to help the animals, rather than go hunting. An owl, returning home in the early dawn from her night adventures, flew about and cried out "What's this? What's happening?"

instead of her usual "Who? Who?" but with an unspoken sign from Goose Steven she fell silent. Beavers lumbered purposefully onto the shoreline and forest birds settled in rows upon tree branches. Some animals remained deep in the forest still afraid to approach the lake, but they remained alert and ready to recite the verse on a signal.

In the meantime, Miranda continued her watch by Smog Dragon who, not suspecting that his days were numbered, noisily banged his tail and snored loudly.

They began to notice the change that occurred all around them. Majestic trees, clean water, tall juicy grass and other forest treasures, which were there before Smog Dragon took up residence, were returning!

"Look," whispered a little squirrel "the forest is coming back to us."

"And the lake, just look at the clean water and all the fish dancing in it," marveled the beaver.

The sun rose higher, spreading its light over Crystal Lake so that all who had come, running, crawling, hopping or flying, could join forces to chase off Smog Dragon. It was time to begin. Rainbow Captain gave a sign and all the inhabitants of Crystal Lake and the forest dwellers called out the enchanted words in one great voice:

> *Rainbow, Rainbow, return to the sky;*
>
> *Chase away the Smoggy Dragon;*
>
> *Then the forest will be green;*
>
> *The water crystal clean;*
>
> *The air fresh and light;*
>
> *And the sun forever bright.*

They gazed at the sky, but there was no change. Rainbow Captain gave the sign again, and again everyone cried even more loudly:

Rainbow, Rainbow, return to the sky;

Chase away the Smoggy Dragon;

Then the forest will be green;

The water crystal clean;

The air fresh and light;

And the sun forever bright.

They studied the sky, but everything remained exactly the same. Then the Rainbow Captain waved his hand and all who were gathered around the lake, or flying in the sky, or hiding in the bushes cried out with all their hearts:

Rainbow, Rainbow, return to the sky;

Chase away the Smoggy Dragon;

then the forest will be green;

The water crystal clean;

The air fresh and light;

And the sun forever bright.

Suddenly a thunderous crackle split the sky and a rainbow of extraordinary beauty emerged like a colorful bridge thrown from one edge of the sky to the other. And nearer still, a fearful splintering sound was heard, followed by a quaking rumble which grew to a deafening roar. Gleeful smiles that had greeted nature's renewal and the rainbow were turned to masks of fear.

As the terrible noise magnified, the bewildered animals saw Miranda racing for her life away from a plume of black smoke that rose from the direction of Smog Dragon's lair. Behind her, clumps of earth, rocks and broken branches hurtled into the air. The magic was starting to work. The

crowded Crystal Lake dwellers gazed in mute astonishment as pieces of Smog Dragon were blown into the sky on tongues of flame and billows of smoke. As Rainbow Captain, Big White Cloud and Goose Steven dashed toward Miranda, everybody rejoiced.

The flock of wild geese took to the sky, honking and squawking with delight. Birds sang songs of triumph and butterflies twirled round and round in dizzy rainbow merry-go-rounds. From the clear-blue sky, a sparkling shower fell, and the pure rainwater washed Smog Dragon's remains into the earth.

The dwellers rushed to the Dragon's lair.

A small dirty patch on the ground was the only reminder of Dragon. There was nothing left of the terrible mess and the land around was covered by new flowers and fresh green grass.

"Friends!" shouted Rainbow Captain, "the ugly monster is gone! We've won!"

"We've won!" cried the birds and beasts.

"We've won!" resounded the forest echo.

"We've won!" swished the tender green grass.

Then the jubilant dwellers of Crystal Lake and the green forest began to dance, and they danced three days and three nights without stopping.

The birds flew to all the corners of the world singing the news of the victory wherever they went. The news was taken to the cliff where Bald Eagle sat, and the sea where Merry Dolphin swam. When Trout Gordon learned that Smog Dragon was dead, he swam back home to his friends. Even the monkeys in the jungle, Pink Flamingo and Dreaded Python were told the happy news. When Cat Lawrence heard of the victory he hastened to Zaki the Golden Lion and gave him a full report about the event.

"I'm not surprised," growled Zaki, "I knew they would get rid of that wicked monster on Crystal Lake. Whenever you want something very badly and put all your effort into it, you are sure to win in the end."

You know my friend, that's what I think too.

..............Glossary

Atmosphere is the air that surrounds us all

Commitment when you hang in there no matter what

Cosmos is anywhere you would go in a rocket ship

Dignity is what makes you a really true person

Environment is what surrounds you every step you make and every
breath you take

Farewell good-bye

Funnel a not-much-fun spinning tube of wind

Galaxy a giant cinnamon bun of stars

Infinity endlessness

Liana vines jungle plants looking like bungie cords

Maneuver like zig-zagging around on a skate board

Noble being super cool whether you feel like it or not

Stratosphere is the last stop in the atmosphere before entering outer
space

Subordinate is a person who gets bossed around

Twister a funnel storm that works like a giant vacuum cleaner

To volunteer to do something helpful for nothing and feel good
about it